THE PRINCE AND THE PAUPER

Mark Twain

Adapted by
Shirley Bogart

Illustrations by Brendan Lynch

BARONET BOOKS, New York, New York

GREAT ILLUSTRATED CLASSICS

edited by
Malvina G. Vogel

Contents

About the Author

Mark Twain was born Samuel Clemens, November 30, 1835, in Florida, Missouri. When he was four, his father, an unsuccessful storekeeper, decided to move his family to Hannibal, Missouri.

This move had a strong effect on Samuel's life. Hannibal was a river-edge town through which many travelers passed: circus troupes, minstrel shows, religious leaders, and daring settlers on their way to California—all of whom Samuel would later use as characters in his books.

But of all the people young Samuel met, he admired the steamboat captains most of all, and dearly wished he could pilot a Mississippi riverboat. Upon his father's death, when Samuel was 12, he left school to train as a printer. This led to newspaper writing out

West and finally the realizing of his dream—for four proud years, he navigated a steamboat up the winding Mississippi River. From this experience, he chose his pen name, "Mark Twain," which in navigation is the call to report the depth of water at two fathoms.

Mark Twain is best known for his funny story, "The Celebrated Jumping Frog of Calaveras County," and for his novels, both humorous and serious. The most famous of these are *The Adventures of Tom Sawyer, The Adventures of Huckleberry Finn, A Connecticut Yankee in King Arthur's Court,* and *The Prince and the Pauper.* In this last book, he poked fun at the old upper-class in England, and showed how wrong it was to judge people by outward appearances.

Mark Twain died in April, 1910, but to his many readers around the world, he will live forever in Tom Sawyer, Huckleberry Finn, Tom Canty, Edward Tudor, and his other unforgettable characters.

Born on the Same Day

CHAPTER 1

Two Different Worlds

One autumn day in the 1500s, two babies were born. Both were boys, both had the same birthday, and both were born in London, England. Aside from those facts, life couldn't have been more different for the two.

Tom Canty was born to a family who wore raggedy clothes and lived in one crowded room. To them, the newborn was just another unwelcome mouth to feed.

Edward Tudor, on the other hand, was born in a palace, to a family who went wild with joy at his birth. So did all of England, for Edward was a prince. Cared for by great lords and ladies, little Prince Edward slept through the noisy street parties and bonfires in his honor.

Tom Canty's street, Offal Court, was noisy too, and crowded and dirty as well. His family lived on the third floor of a rickety house. His fifteen-year-old twin sisters, Bet and Nan, were good-natured like their mother. But his father and grandmother, Gammer Canty, were absolute terrors. He stole and she cursed. And both drank and fought a lot.

John Canty would roar at his family, "Where is the stuff from today's begging?"

Mrs. Canty would timidly hand him the coin she had gotten, and one of the girls would come up with a chunk of stale bread.

Then John Canty would turn to Tom. "What about you, brat? Nothing!" And he would grab his son and smack him around hard.

Then the grandmother would shriek at Tom, "I'm ashamed to call a rotten good-for-nothing like you my grandson!" And she would give him another beating.

"What About You, Brat?"

THE PRINCE AND THE PAUPER

Late at night, Tom would lie sobbing and hungry on a pile of dirty straw under a scrap of blanket. He would hear his name whispered and feel a bit of crust slipped into his hand.

"No, Ma, it's *yours*," he would protest. "You haven't had any supper either."

Then a roar would come. "WHAT'S THIS? Spoil the no-good brat, will you?"

Tom would freeze as his father hit his mother, while Gammer Canty cackled through her toothless gums, "It serves you right!"

Oddly enough, Tom wasn't an unhappy boy. Everyone around him had the same kind of life, so he thought that his was normal. Besides, he had a special friend, Father Andrew.

The poor priest lived in another part of the rickety house and secretly taught some of the neighborhood children. He not only taught them right from wrong, but reading and writing as well. Tom was an eager student and soon began to study Latin too. Through the stories the old priest told him and from the

"No, Ma, It's *Yours.*"

books he read, Tom learned about kings and princes. Their lives never ceased to amaze the young boy.

"And do they really wear different clothes every day?" he asked Father Andrew.

"Yes, indeed, Tom. Made of rich cloth and always clean too."

"My rags are cleaner lately, and so am I."

"I've noticed the change, and a good one it is. But where in the world do you find enough water to wash them?"

"It's easy, Father. After playing in the mud with my friends, I go down to the Thames River and splash about till I'm clean."

Then with shining, eager eyes, he pleaded, "Please, Father, tell me again how the king commands his council."

"You never tire of those stories, do you, Tom? But with all the reading you've done, I think *you're* the expert on royal ways now."

It was true. Tom knew so much about royal life that he even began to sound and act like a

Father Andrew's Eager Pupil

king, much to the amazement of his friends. His words were so intelligent and his decisions so wise that even some grown-ups came to him for advice, and came away impressed with the boy.

After a while, Tom formed his friends into a make-believe court, with himself at the head. He issued orders to his "guards" and "lords and ladies-in-waiting." He held meetings of the "royal council" and gave commands to the "heads of the army and navy."

But that was not enough for Tom Canty. Just once in his life, he longed to see a real prince. The longing was with him while he begged for scraps of food, while he got his beatings, and even while he slept. All of his dreams were set in a dazzling court, where glittering lords and ladies murmured to him as he breathed perfumed air and heard heavenly music.

Then he would wake up to the ugliness around him, and cry.

Tom's Make-Believe Court

Outside the Palace Gates

CHAPTER 2

The Big Switch

One day, Tom awoke and went out, hungry as usual. He was so wrapped up in his dreams of the night before, that as he wandered about the city, he didn't notice where he was going. When he found himself before an enormous building with a stone gateway, gold bars, and huge stone lions—the sign of royalty, he knew that it could only be a king's palace.

"Perhaps now, at long last, I'll get my chance to see a real prince," he whispered.

As the ragged boy approached the golden bars, he glimpsed inside a sun-tanned boy in clothes of silk and satin sprinkled with sparkling jewels. Near him stood several well-dressed men. "His servants," Tom told himself.

His eyes wide with wonder and delight, Tom drew closer to the bars. Then suddenly, a soldier in armor snatched him away and pushed him into the crowd of townspeople who always gathered to gaze at the palace.

"Mind your, manners, you little beggar!" shouted the soldier.

The crowd laughed at poor Tom, but the prince had seen the soldier's action and came running.

"How dare you!" he cried. "How dare you treat even the lowest of my father's subjects that way! Open the gate and let him in!"

Waving the guards aside and taking Tom's hand, Edward Tudor led the ragged boy into the palace.

"You look tired and hungry," he said. "You look like you have been treated badly."

Tom could only look around him in wonder

The Prince Comes to Tom's Aid.

as the prince led him into a richly decorated room he called his cabinet. Then he ordered a servant to bring Tom some food. It was just about the fanciest feast the boy could have ever imagined.

The prince sent his servants away so that Tom could have some privacy while he ate and so that they could talk freely.

First, Edward asked Tom his name and where he lived and about the Canty family.

"I have parents and twin sisters, Nan and Bet," said Tom. "And a grandmother, but I don't like her."

"I take it she isn't too kind to you?"

"She isn't kind to anyone. She has a wicked heart and evil ways."

"Does she mistreat you much?"

"Well, there are times when she doesn't, but that's only when she's asleep or drunk. But once her head is clear again, she makes up for it with some pretty good beatings."

"Beatings!" cried Edward. "Why, I'll have

The Fanciest Feast Ever Imagined!

her sent to the Tower of London prison."

"No, Your Majesty. You forget—the Tower is only for noble or important prisoners."

"Oh, yes. I hadn't thought of that. . . . Then I'll think of some other punishment. Now, how does your father treat you?"

"The same as Gammer," replied Tom.

"Maybe all fathers are alike," said the prince. "Mine has a pretty bad temper too. He doesn't hit me, but he scolds me plenty. . . ."

"What about your mother?"

"She is a good person. So are my sisters."

"How old are they?"

"Fifteen."

"My sister, Lady Elizabeth, is fourteen, and I've got a cousin my age, Lady Jane Grey. Say, do your sisters keep telling their servants not to smile because smiling's a sin?"

"Oh, Your Highness, do you think my sisters have servants?"

"Of course. Otherwise, who helps them undress at night? And who dresses them when

Asking Tom Questions

they get up in the morning?"

"Nobody. You don't expect them to take their dress off and sleep with nothing on, as the animals do!"

"Their *dress?*" cried the prince in disbelief. "Do you mean to tell me they have only one dress apiece?"

"Certainly, Your Majesty. Why would they need more than one dress? They have only got one body apiece."

Prince Edward laughed, then apologized for doing so. "I promise that your good sisters will soon have enough clothes."

Tom tried to thank the prince, but Edward would not permit it. Instead, he seemed to want to hear more about Offal Court. "What do you do there all day?" Edward asked.

"There's a traveling puppet show to watch, and entertainers with monkeys. Then there are plays with lots of shouting, fighting, and killing. It costs only a farthing to see these shows, but a farthing is hard to get."

A Puppet Show in Offal Court

THE PRINCE AND THE PAUPER

"Tell me more," the prince said eagerly. "What do you do with your friends?"

"We sometimes have stick fights and we run races. In the summer, we go wading in the canals. We have water battles in the river, splashing each other all over the place."

"How I would love that!" cried Edward. "If only I could do those things—just once! But go on."

"And at the river's edge, we bury each other in the sand and make mud pies with lovely, oozing mud. There's nothing like it for fun in the whole world."

"Oh, please," interrupted Edward, "don't tell me any more! If only I could dress in clothes like yours and swoosh around in the mud barefoot, with no one to scold me! I think I'd give up the crown for that!"

"And I wish, just once, that I could be dressed like you and. . . ."

"Do you really? All right, then. You take off your things and put on mine. We'll change

Water Battles in the River

clothes for a little while, then switch back before anyone bothers us."

In a few minutes, Edward, Prince of Wales, was in rags. And Tom Canty, the beggar boy—the pauper—was in royal clothing. When the two boys stood side by side before a full-length mirror, both were astonished. The change seemed not to have taken place at all!

"Amazing!" cried the prince. "We have the same hair, the same eyes, the same build, the same voice and manner. Nobody could really tell us apart. Nobody could say which of us was the prince and which was the pauper."

Tom nodded, too amazed to speak.

"And now that I'm in your clothes," continued Edward, "I can feel as you did when my soldier pushed you. I say, isn't that a bruise on your hand?"

"It is nothing, Your Majesty."

"Nothing! It was a cruel thing!" cried Edward, stamping his bare foot. "I'm going out to give that soldier a good scolding. Now don't

"Nobody Could Really Tell Us Apart."

move from this room till I return."

Quickly putting away a large, round gold disc that had been on the table, the prince dashed outside. At the gate, he grabbed the bars and shouted, "Open! Unbar the gates!"

The same soldier who had hurt Tom obeyed at once and, as Edward ran out angrily, the soldier gave the boy a hard smack on the ear. Edward was sent whirling into the roadway as the crowd outside roared with laughter.

"That's for getting me in trouble with His Highness!" called the soldier.

"You'll hang for laying your hands on me!" cried Edward, picking himself out of the mud. "I'm the Prince of Wales!"

"Oh, so sorry, Your Majesty," mocked the soldier. "I salute your gracious Highness—now get out of here, you crazy beggar!"

The hooting crowd closed in around the prince, pushing him away from the palace and chanting, "Make way for His Royal Highness!"

"Get Out of Here, You Crazy Beggar!"

Sad and Bewildered and Lost

CHAPTER 3

A Prince Among Paupers

Nobody in the crowd believed that this ragged creature who called himself the Prince of Wales was really Edward Tudor. But they followed him for hours to laugh at his royal commands.

Finally, tired of their fun, they left him to wander the streets of London, sad and bewildered and lost. Suddenly his hopes rose. He recognized a building where he felt sure he could get help. It was Christ's Church Hospital—a home that his own father had set up for poor and abandoned boys.

He approached a crowd of boys who were

running and jumping and playing ball and leapfrog. They stopped their noisy games to stare at the prince.

"Good lads," said Edward, "tell your master that Edward, Prince of Wales, is here."

"Hah! What are you, beggar, the prince's messenger?" sneered a tall boy.

Edward's Hand automatically went to his hip, but nothing was there.

"Hey, look at that!" said another boy. "He thought he had a sword, just like the prince."

Again everybody hooted, which made Edward even angrier. "I *am* the prince," he cried, "and it's wrong for you to treat me this way when you are here because of the kindness of my father, the king."

This remark set the boys roaring, and the tall boy pretended to scold his friends. "What's wrong with you, lowly swine? You who live off his father! Get down on your knees to his Royal Ragship!"

The boys obeyed, making a show of

"On Your Knees to His Royal Ragship!"

honoring Edward. But the prince kicked the boy nearest him.

"Now he's gone too far!" said one.

"Drag him to the pond!" yelled another.

"And let's get the dogs!" called a third.

Never before in the history of England had the royal heir to the throne been roughed up by common hands and set upon by dogs.

By the end of the day, Edward found himself in the crowded center of the city, bruised, bleeding, muddy, and exhausted. As he wandered helplessly, he kept telling himself, "I must get to Offal Court before I faint. Tom Canty's people will know I'm not their son and will take me back to the palace."

Then he thought of the boys who had mistreated him, and he decided, "When I am king, I will make sure the boys at Christ's Hospital have more than food, clothes, and shelter. They need an education too, to soften their hearts and bring kindness to their lives."

He was making his way through a noisy,

Set Upon by Boys and Dogs!

winding alley in the cold rain when a drunken ruffian grabbed him by the collar.

"Why are you out so late and where are the farthings you earned?" growled a rough voice. "I'm going to break every bone in your body, or my name isn't John Canty!"

The prince wriggled loose happily. "Oh, you're John Canty!" he cried. "You're his father. That's wonderful!"

"*His* father? What are you babbling about? All I know is I'm *your* father, and you'll catch it good when —"

"Please, good sir, do not joke now. I cannot take any more. I am tired and wounded. Just get me to my father, the king, and he will make you richer than your wildest dreams."

"You've gone *mad*!" John Canty cried, roughly grabbing him again. "But crazy or not, your Gammer Canty and I will soon bruise your bones as well as your brains!"

With that, he dragged the struggling prince away, as a noisy, swarming crowd followed.

"Where Are the Farthings You Earned?"

In Front of the Great Mirror

CHAPTER 4

The Pauper as a Prince

Meanwhile, back at the palace, Tom was enjoying parading in front of the great mirror bowing and flourishing the jeweled dagger. He had fun trying out all the richly upholstered chairs and wondering what people at Offal Court would say if they could see him now.

After about an hour, when the prince hadn't returned, a frightening thought hit Tom. What if someone came in and saw him dressed in the prince's clothes, with Edward not there to explain? They might hang him first and ask questions later.

He began pacing nervously, fearing every sound he heard. Soon the door opened and a

41

page announced, "The Lady Jane Grey."

A pretty blonde girl in a fur-trimmed velvet dress came bounding in. Then, seeing his expression, she stopped. "My Lord," she said with concern, "what is the matter?"

"I-I'm not a lord," Tom managed to stammer as he fell to his knees. "I'm simply poor Tom Canty from Offal Court. I beg you, let me see the prince so that he may give me back my rags and let me leave here safely."

"Oh, Your Highness!" cried the horror-stricken girl. "You shouldn't be kneeling to *me*!" And she turned and fled.

Soon the word spread through the palace, from servant to servant and from lord to lord "The prince has gone mad!"

When word reached the king, he immediately issued an order that no one was to repeat that rumor, under penalty of death. And the whispering suddenly stopped.

Two nobles and the court doctor were sent to Tom, and they accompanied him to an elegant

"You Shouldn't Be Kneeling to *Me*!"

apartment of the palace. Before him sat a fat, gray-haired man with a stern-looking face. This was the king, the dreaded Henry VIII. One of his swollen legs was wrapped in bandages and rested on a pillow.

Every head in the room was bowed before the king, but his face grew gentle as he looked at Tom.

"Well now, Edward, what's this I hear? Are you trying to make fun of me—me, the king and your father, who loves you?"

"The king!" cried Tom, falling to his knees. "Now I'm doomed!"

Hearing this, King Henry seemed stunned. "Then it is true . . . the rumors I heard. Come to me. Do you not know who I am, son?"

"Oh, yes, Your Majesty," said Tom as he approached Henry. "You're the king, and I'm just a poor boy here by accident, and much too young to die. Won't you save me, please?"

"Die? Of course you won't die." And he took Tom's curly head and pressed it gently to his chest.

Meeting King Henry VIII

THE PRINCE AND THE PAUPER

"Bless you, Your Highness!" cried Tom, falling to his knees. Then he jumped up and turned to the nobles. "You heard the king. I am not to die!" he cried joyously.

The nobles shook their heads at each other sadly, but no one spoke.

Then the king looked up hopefully. "Maybe he's only *partly* mad," he said. "I'll test him." And he asked the boy a question in Latin.

Tom could answer in that language because of Father Andrew's teachings.

But when it came to French, Tom could not reply, and the king fell back in disappointment. "Never mind," he said with a sigh. "The boy's brain has been temporarily overtaxed with his studies. He'll have no more books or teachers for a while, only wholesome sports until he's well again."

Henry took a breath and continued with feeling. "Mad or not, he is my son, and there is one thing I insist on. He is the Prince of Wales

A Father's Love and Concern

and he shall reign. I want him so installed officially tomorrow. You, Lord Hertford, as his uncle, will see to the arrangements."

"The king's will is law," replied Lord Hertford.

Tom felt like a prisoner now, a prisoner in a golden cage. And he had no way to escape!

Soon after, he was led to a magnificent suite, and Lord St. John was announced.

"I have a private message from the king," he told Tom. "Will Your Lordship dismiss all the others except your uncle from the room."

Tom hesitated. Father Andrew had never told him how to dismiss nobility.

Realizing that the boy was confused, Lord Hertford whispered, "Just wave your hand. You don't have to bother speaking unless you want to."

When the three were alone, Lord St. John said, "His Majesty commands that you are to hide your illness as much as you can. When you think you are someone of low birth, you

"You Are To Hide Your Illness."

are *not* to say so. When you do not understand something you are expected to know, you are to *pretend* to understand. If you are confused in matters of state, you are *not* to show it. Instead, you are to look to Lord Hertford or myself for advice. We are commanded to stay close to you until God makes you well."

"I shall obey the king," said Tom quietly.

How he would abide by these orders was soon tested, when his sister, Princess Elizabeth, and Lady Jane were announced. As they entered, Lord Hertford whispered to them, "Do not let on if he acts strangely or forgets things."

All went well until Lady Jane asked, "Have you visited your mother, the queen, today?"

Tom looked upset and would have blurted out anything when Lord St. John saved him. "Yes, he did," replied the nobleman, "and they discussed the king's poor health."

Tom mumbled some agreement and was safe until a bit later when Lady Jane said, "What a

Lord St. John Answers for Tom.

shame you have stopped studying. You were doing so well, My Prince. You'll probably learn as many languages as your father."

"My father!" cried Tom without thinking. "The way *he* talks *his own language*, only the pigs in their stys can understand him. And as for any kind of learning—"

A warning look in Lord St. John's eyes stopped him.

"I'm sorry," he said. "It is my sickness again. My mind must have wandered."

"That's all right," said Princess Elizabeth, patting his hand. "It's not your fault."

The time with the two girls passed pleasantly, and Tom grew more at ease. So when Lord Hertford reminded him that he would need to rest before a banquet that evening and when the girls announced that they were looking forward to it, Tom relieved and delighted. At least he would know *two* people there!

"My Mind Must Have Wandered."

THE PRINCE AND THE PAUPER

It was then that the princess asked, "Have we the permission of my brother, the Prince, to leave?"

"Your Ladyships can have anything in the world that is in my power to give," Tom answered. "But it saddens me to lose your pleasant company."

Tom smiled at his own words and thought, "It was not in vain, then, that I did all that reading on royal ways and gracious speech."

When the girls had gone, Tom announced that he wished to rest. A nobleman was summoned to lead Tom to an inner apartment.

As Tom reached for a cup of water, a servant snatched it, dropped to one knee, and offered it on a golden tray. When Tom bent to take his shoes off, another servant dropped to his knees and did it for him.

After two or three more such attempts to undress himself, Tom finally gave up. "It is a wonder they don't try to breathe for me too," he murmured.

Servants for Everything!

A Princely Dinner Begins.

CHAPTER 5

Make Way for the High and Mighty

At about one o'clock that afternoon, the servants began to dress Tom for dinner. Everything was changed from his ruff—his stiff lace collar, to his shoes. He underwent the ordeal of being dressed with resignation.

Tom was then led in a procession to a huge dining room and was seated at a solid gold table elegantly set for one. As the hungry boy prepared to devour the food, the Royal Diaperer sprang forward and quickly fastened a napkin around Tom's neck. As he was about to pour himself a cup of wine, the Royal Cup-Bearer stepped up to do it for him. Tom looked around in wonderment, never suspecting that these were only part of the prince's personal staff of 384 servants!

Because the servants had been warned not to show surprise at any odd behavior by the prince, nobody laughed when Tom ate with his fingers, nor when he pulled his napkin off, inspected it, then said, "Take this beautiful thing away. I'm afraid I'll dirty it."

All they saw was that their beloved prince was ill. And this saddened, not amused them.

After his dessert, Tom filled his pockets with nuts, then realized that this was the only part of the meal he had been allowed to pick up for himself. So when his nose began to itch, he wondered if it would be princely to scratch it with his own hands.

He tried to ignore the twitching, but the itch got so bad that tears came to his eyes. Two lords sprang forward to ask what was the matter. When Tom tearfully explained about the itch, they were perplexed.

Is It Princely To Scratch One's Nose?

THE PRINCE AND THE PAUPER

"There is no Royal Scratcher of the Royal Nose!" cried one lord. "What are we to do?"

At last, the twitching nose became too much for Tom and, with a silent prayer for forgiveness if he was doing wrong, he reached up and scratched—an act that brought relief to all the courtiers in the room.

When the meal was over, a lord presented a golden fingerbowl with sweet-smelling rosewater for the prince to clean his mouth and hands. The Royal Diaperer stood ready with a napkin. Tom stared at the dish, puzzled, then slowly lifted it to his lips, and took a sip.

"Thank you, my Lord," he said, putting down the bowl. "It has a pretty scent, but not much taste."

The courtiers' hearts ached at the prince's madness, and nobody laughed at that, or at Tom's next mistake—getting up and leaving the table just as the chaplain posted himself behind the royal chair, with eyes closed and arms uplifted, to begin the blessing.

Lifting the Fingerbowl to His Lips

THE PRINCE AND THE PAUPER

Alone in his room, Tom amused himself by trying on parts of a suit of armor and by cracking and eating the nuts. For the first time, Tom began to enjoy the role of prince.

Then an unexpected discovery made him even happier—some books on proper etiquette in the English court. Tom made himself comfortable on the couch and began to do some heavy studying.

Meanwhile, King Henry's illness was getting more serious. Fearing that he was dying Henry decided that one of his last acts would be to seal the doom of his political enemy, the Duke of Norfolk, now imprisoned in the Tower of London.

"I want him beheaded, and I will give the order now," Henry announced from his bed to the Lord Chancellor. "Fetch me the Great Royal Seal to place on the order."

"The Seal?" asked the Lord Chancellor "But, Your Majesty, you have the Seal."

"Well, I don't have it now. . . . Where can it

A Last Political Act

be? . . . My memory is playing tricks on me these days. . . ."

"Sire, I believe you gave it to your son, the prince," offered Lord Hertford.

"True, true. . . . I remember now," mumbled the king. "Go and fetch it."

A short while later, Lord Hertford returned, empty-handed, explaining, "I fear that the prince's illness is on him again, and he doesn't remember your giving him the Seal."

"Don't bother the poor lad anymore," said the king sadly. "We'll use the small Royal Seal then. But the Duke of Norfolk dies tomorrow!"

At nine that evening, the riverfront of the palace was lit up with lanterns and torches. The boats and barges on the water were adorned with banners and silken flags and little silver bells that shook out tiny showers of music with every breeze.

There were crowds of spectators: men-at-arms in glossy helmets and breastplates,

The Riverfront Is Lit Up.

brilliantly dressed musicians, and noblemen and ladies in colorful finery.

A flourish of trumpets sounded, and Lord Hertford came through a gateway, magnificent in a red satin cape over a black and gold doublet. "Make way for the High and Mighty Lord Edward, Prince of Wales!" he called, bowing at each step.

A long trumpet blast followed. The masses burst into a mighty roar of welcome as Tom Canty, elegantly dressed, stepped forward and bowed. His purple tunic was powdered with diamonds and edged with ermine. His long, white cloth-of-gold cape, embroidered with the three-feathered Tudor crest and set with pearls and precious stones, was fastened with a clasp of colorful gems. Gold medals of honor hung from his neck, their jewels flashing whenever the light fell on them.

This, then, was the spectacle surrounding young Tom Canty—the gutter boy accustomed only to dirt and rags!

"Make Way for the Prince of Wales!"

Trying Unsuccessfully To Stop a Beating

CHAPTER 6

Lost in the Crowd

Clearly, Tom Canty had come a long way from his starting place, Offal Court—this same filthy alley where the true Prince Edward now found himself being dragged by the drunken bully, John Canty.

As the dragging and beating continued, only one man tried to stop John Canty. But Canty hit him over the head with his stick, and the man sank to the ground.

Once inside the Canty apartment, Edward peered through the weak light of a candle stuck in a bottle to see two frowsy girls and a middle-aged woman clinging to a corner wall. Canty ignored them and spoke to a wrinkled old hag with straggly gray hair and evil eyes, who stood in another corner. "Get ready for a fine show, Gammer. But don't interrupt now. You can get him later. . . . Step forward, boy. Now say it again. What's your name?"

Edward, unaccustomed to such insults, stared up at Canty and indignantly replied, "You are rude to command me to speak. But I will tell you again—I am Edward, Prince of Wales, and no other."

The answer was so unexpected that Gammer Canty stood as if nailed to the floor. Her son thought her amazement so comical that he burst into a roar of laughter.

But Tom's mother and sisters were so distressed at his apparent madness, they ran to him, crying, "Oh, poor Tom! Poor lad!"

The mother knelt before him and gazed sadly into his face. "Why didn't you listen when I warned you?" she sobbed. "All that foolish reading has scrambled your brains!"

Canty Roars at Edward's Words.

THE PRINCE AND THE PAUPER

The prince answered gently, "Rest easy, good lady. Your son is fine and hasn't lost his mind. Let me get to the palace, where he is, and my father, the king, will send him back to you."

This answer brought on a fresh outburst from the woman. "The king, your father? Oh, shake off that wild dream, Tom, and look at me. Am I not your mother?"

The prince shook his head sadly. "I'm sorry to hurt you," he said, "but the truth is I have never seen your face before in my life."

The poor woman sank to the floor, sobbing.

But John Canty yelled, "On with the show! Come on, Nan, and you too, Bet, you ill-mannered brats. Get down on your knees in the presence of the prince!" And he gave another hoarse laugh.

"Please, Father," pleaded Nan, "let him go to bed now."

"Yes, Father," added Bet. "Tomorrow he'll go out to beg and bring in some money."

"Am I Not Your Mother?"

THE PRINCE AND THE PAUPER

"Tomorrow we must pay the rent on this hole, or out we go," yelled John Canty to the boy. "Now show me what you got with your lazy begging!"

"Do not insult the king's son with such lowly matters," said Edward.

John Canty's reply was a punch in the shoulder that sent the prince staggering. Mrs. Canty caught him and shielded him with her body from the rain of blows that followed.

The two frightened girls shrank back, but the grandmother stepped forward eagerly to help her son.

The prince sprang away from Mrs. Canty, saying, "No, you won't take the blows for me, madam. Let these swine attack me alone."

That was all the evil pair had to hear, and they began to beat the boy soundly, then added more blows on the mother and sisters for showing him sympathy.

"Now get to bed, all of you," said Canty. "The entertainment has tired me out."

Mrs. Canty Catches Edward.

THE PRINCE AND THE PAUPER

Once the lights were out and Gammer and her son were snoring, Nan and Bet crept over to Edward and covered him tenderly with straw and rags. Mrs. Canty stroked his hair and whispered words of comfort.

The prince thanked them gratefully and begged them to go to sleep, promising them that the king would reward their kindness.

That night, Mrs. Canty found herself wondering, "What if the boy really *isn't* my son?" The idea haunted her until she hit on a test to find out for sure.

When the prince gave a startled cry in his sleep, she remembered that, as a baby, Tom had once been frightened by a sudden burst of gunpowder. From that time on, anything that startled him always caused him to throw his hand in front of his eyes in an unusual way— with the palm out. This would be the test.

Mrs. Canty held a lit candle before the sleeping boy and rapped on the floor beside his head. His eyes sprang open, but he made no

Mrs. Canty's Test

movement with his hands. So she repeated it a second and third time.

"It can't be," she told herself sadly. "A person's *mind* may go mad, but not his *hands*. My son could not have given up that lifelong habit. No, that boy is *not* my Tom!"

At this moment, there came a loud knocking at the door. John Canty stopped snoring and called out, "Who's there? What do you want?"

A voice answered, "Do you know who you flattened in the street last night?"

"No, and I don't care!" Canty roared back.

"You'll care all right when you hear this. It happens to be the priest, Father Andrew and he's dying!"

"God-a-mercy!" exclaimed Canty. "Everybody up and run for your lives!"

Within minutes, the household was out in the dark of night, flying through the streets, with John Canty gripping Edward's wrist.

"Mind your tongue, mad fool," he said to the boy, "and don't speak the name Canty.

"Everybody Up and Run for Your Lives!"

I don't want the law on our trail."

To the rest of the family he growled, "If we get separated, we'll meet at the last linen shop on London Bridge. From there, we'll cross the river together to Southwark."

But Canty hadn't counted on the celebration going on at the riverfront. Fireworks, singing, and dancing filled the streets, as all of London made merry. In no time at all the family was caught up by the crowds and parted, except for John Canty and Edward, who were held together by the man's firm grip on the boy's wrist.

As he pushed through the crowd, Canty jostled a huge boatman, who grabbed his arm and snapped, "What's your rush?"

This left Edward free for a split second. In that second, he dove among the legs surrounding him and disappeared into the crowd, determined to make his way to Guildhall, where he would resume his true place . . . and hang Tom Canty for treason!

"What's Your Rush?"

Tom Marches to the Guildhall.

CHAPTER 7

The Kingdom of Dreams and Shadows

Tom, too, was heading for the Guildhall, but in rather a different style—on silken cushions in the royal barge. After disembarking, he and his procession made the short march to that ancient town hall.

The Lord Mayor and important city officials bowed and led Tom, Princess Elizabeth, and Lady Jane to the canopy at the front of the enormous hall. Nobles sat at a lower table, and commoners sat lower still.

After the banquet, at midnight, there was a costumed parade, followed by lively dancing.

While Tom sat in his high seat, enjoying the

colorful show, a furious, ragged boy was trying to convince the unruly, taunting crowd outside the hall to let him through.

"I insist I *am* Prince Edward!" he cried, "even if I don't have a single friend on my side to help convince you."

At that moment, a tall, well-built man, dressed in a frayed royal costume with a long sword, pushed through the crowd. "Prince or not," he said, "I like your spirit, lad. From now on, you *do* have a friend in Miles Hendon."

"Hah!" jeered someone in the crowd. "Another prince in disguise. Pull the little beggar from him and toss him into the pond."

But Miles Hendon had drawn his sword from its rusty sheath before anyone could get a hand on the prince. As the mob closed in, he flashed his weapon with the wildness of a madman. Though many victims littered the ground in the sword's path, the rest of the mob came surging forward like a wave, stopping only when a trumpet sounded.

"From Now On, You *Do* Have a Friend."

THE PRINCE AND THE PAUPER

"Make way for the king's messenger!"

As a troop of clattering horsemen charged the crowd, Miles caught the prince up in his arms and fled as fast as his legs could run.

The messenger continued into the Guildhall and again the trumpet sounded. There was instant silence. Then came the announcement: "The king is dead!"

Within the hall, all bowed their heads. Then they dropped to their knees, stretched out their hands to Tom, and burst forth with a great shout: "Long live the king!"

Tom was dazed at first. Then, realizing what was happening, he asked Lord Hertford if his commands would now be obeyed. Assured that they would, the boy said slowly and earnestly, "From this day on, the law of blood is over! The king's law will be the law of mercy. The king decrees that the Duke of Norfolk shall not die!"

As Hertford hurried to the Tower of London

"Long Live the King!"

to carry out the order, another cry broke out in the hall: "The reign of blood is ended! Long live Edward, King of England!"

Miles and the prince headed for the river toward London Bridge, but the news of the death of Henry VIII was on everyone's lips.

Edward was filled with grief, for his father, a tyrant to the world, had always been a gentle person to him. "How strange it seems," he thought. "I am now the king!"

London Bridge was lined with shops and factories and inns—almost a town in itself. And as Miles neared the door of the inn where he lodged, a figure blocked his way.

"So you finally got here!" said a rough voice. "Well, you won't get away again. Not after I pound your bones to pudding!" And John Canty grabbed for the boy.

Miles turned Edward away from him. "Not so fast, my friend. What is the boy to you?"

"If it's any of your business, he's my son," replied Canty.

Canty Grabs for the Boy.

"That's a lie!" shouted the young king.

"Lie or truth," Miles told the boy, "he won't touch you if you prefer to stay with me."

"I do, I do!" cried Edward. "I'd rather die than go with him!"

"Then that's settled. The matter's closed."

"We'll see about that," said Canty, moving toward the boy.

"Just touch him, and I'll split you open like a goose," said Miles, his hand on the hilt of his sword. "Now get moving."

As John Canty moved off, muttering threats and curses, Miles led Edward to his third-floor room, a poor place with one shabby bed, some old furniture, and a few sickly candles.

Edward dragged himself to the bed and lay down, exhausted and hungry. "You may call me when the table is set," he said. But no sooner did his head touch the pillow than he fell into a deep sleep. It was now 2:00 A.M.

Hendon smiled as he bent over the sleeping boy. "He should have been born a prince, he

"I'll Split You Open Like A Goose."

plays the part so well," he thought. And he took off his doublet to cover the small, shivering figure.

Then pacing the room, he muttered, "I will be a friend to the poor little friendless lad, even though he is mad, raving that he is the Prince of Wales. I love the boy, mad as he is— too mad to even realize that he should now take on the title of king."

A servant from the inn, delivering a hot meal Miles had ordered, slammed the door as he left. This woke Edward, who saw himself covered with the doublet.

"You are too good to me," said the boy. "Please put it on again."

Miles did so, then said, "Now let's have a hearty supper."

Edward nodded and walked over to the washstand and waited.

"What's the matter?" asked Miles.

"I'd like to be washed up."

"Go right ahead. Make yourself at home."

Miles Covers the Small, Shivering Figure.

"Will you pour the water and not talk so much!" the boy said, tapping his foot.

Miles tried not to laugh as he did so.

"Come now," snapped Edward, "what about the towel?"

Handing him the towel and leaving the boy to dry himself, Miles, too, washed, then walked over to join Edward at the table.

"Stop!" cried the boy. "Would you sit in the presence of the king?"

"Well, well," thought Miles. "At least his mad brain is aware that he is now king. I'd better humor him or he's liable to order me to the Tower."

So he waited on the boy, treating him in courtly ways.

The meal and the wine made Edward relax a bit, and he asked Miles if he were a nobleman, having noticed his fine manners.

"My father is a baronet, a minor lord, Sir Richard Hendon of Hendon Hall," answered Miles, standing before the boy. "My mother

"I'd Better Humor Him."

died when I was a boy, and I have two brothers."

"What are they like?"

"Arthur, the oldest, is generous like my father. But Hugh, the youngest, is about as mean and vicious a reptile as you can find."

"Are there any others in your family?"

"My cousin, Lady Edith. She was sixteen when I last saw her, and I was twenty. We were deeply in love with each other, but she was promised to Arthur by my father, her guardian, from the time they were babies."

"And did Arthur love her?"

"No. He was anxious to break the marriage contract because he loved somebody else."

"What about Hugh? Did he love her?"

"The only thing Hugh loved was her money. She was an heiress, you see. But he claimed he loved her. And my father believed him.

"Hugh was his favorite, being the youngest. My father even believed all of Hugh's lies when he tried to get me out of the way so he

"We Were Deeply In Love."

could get my share of our inheritance."

"How did he do that?"

"By planting a ladder in my room and convincing my father that I planned to carry Edith off and marry her."

"Your father must have been furious."

"He was. He ordered me away from home. Three years of service in the foreign wars, he said, would make a man of me."

"And did you actually serve in the army?"

"That I did. In my last battle, I was taken prisoner. Seven long years I was away from home before I managed to win my freedom. So here I am now, poor in purse, poor in dress, and poorest of all in not knowing what went on at Hendon Hall all these years. . . ."

"You have been shamefully abused," cried Edward. "But I will right your wrongs."

Then, fired by Miles' story, Edward related his own misfortunes, beginning with exchanging clothes with the beggar boy.

"What a lively imagination!" thought Miles.

Ordered Away from Home

THE PRINCE AND THE PAUPER

"Lively . . . or crazy!"

"Good sir," continued Edward, "you have saved my life, and so my crown. The king invites you now to name your own reward."

Miles played along with Edward, realizing that *one* situation simply could not continue. Dropping to his knees, he said, "Your Majesty, the only reward that I and my heirs beg for is the privilege of *sitting* in the presence of England's Royal Majesty."

The king took Hendon's sword and tapped him lightly on the shoulder with it. "Rise, Sir Miles Hendon, Knight," he said solemnly. "Rise and be seated. Your petition is granted, so long as England lives."

"And a good thing too," said Miles to himself, dropping into a chair. "My legs were getting awfully tired. . . . I only hope he doesn't call me a knight in front of other people, for I am merely a Knight of the Kingdom of Dreams and Shadows—the dreams and shadows of the lad's madness!"

"Rise, Sir Miles Hendon, Knight."

Tom's Wonderful Dream

CHAPTER 8

A Strange Job

Meanwhile, Tom Canty, asleep in the palace, was having a wonderful dream about going home again, with money for his mother and Nan and Bet and Father Andrew, when suddenly a voice said, "It grows late, Your Majesty. May it please you to rise?"

The dream faded, and with it Tom's hopes of getting home again—he was still a captive . . . and a king. Now he would have to go through the ridiculous process of being dressed by the Royal Lord of the Bedchamber.

Each garment, from shirt down to shoes, was inspected and passed along through fourteen nobles, ending with the First Lord of the Bedchamber, who got to put it on Tom. If anything was less than perfect, like a pulled thread on a stocking, back it went hand to hand, and a replacement passed along.

Finally, after the proper lord poured wash water, the proper lord handed a towel, and the Hairdresser-Royal did his work, Tom stood as pretty as a girl, in a purple cape, purple suit, and a purple-plumed hat.

After breakfast, he was taken to the throne room, where he listened to business reports and to requests for audiences with the king. Always, Lord Hertford stood at his side, whispering advice.

Poor Tom found it all very boring and wondered, "What did I ever do wrong, that God should take me out of the fresh air and sunshine and coop me up here to be a king?"

Then a newcomer entered, a boy of about twelve, dressed all in black. He knelt down.

"Rise, young man. What do you want?"

Passing Each Garment to the Bedchamber Lord

"Surely you remember me, Your Grace. I am Humphrey Marlowe, your whipping-boy."

Tom frowned. A whipping-boy was one court person he knew nothing about. With Hertford having left the room on business, Tom decided that the best way to find out was to plead his illness. Slowly, he stroked his forehead. "You must help me, Humphrey," he said. "You know I have this illness that has damaged my memory. . . . I seem to remember you now, but you have to give me a clue about your business here."

"Certainly, Your Majesty. Two days ago, you made three mistakes during your Greek lesson, remember?"

"I do recall it now. Go on."

"Well, your tutor, being angry with such careless work, said he would have to whip me for it."

"Whip *you*? Why you, if it was my fault?"

"Ah, Your Grace forgets again. He *always* hits me when you fail in your lessons. After

106

"You Have To Give Me a Clue."

all, no one may hit the sacred body of the Prince of Wales. So when he errs, *I* get hit instead. That's only right—it's my job."

"And did you get that promised beating?"

"No, Your Majesty. It was supposed to be for today, but because of the mourning period, I was wondering if you might wish to —"

"Cancel the whipping? Of course!"

"Thank you, my Lord." The boy hesitated, and kneeled again. "I probably have asked for enough, and yet . . . now that Your Majesty is king, I'm worried that you will be giving up your studies. My job will be gone, and my orphan sisters and I will starve!"

"Your worries are over. The job will be in your family forever." And he tapped the boy's shoulder with the flat of his sword. "Rise, Humphrey Marlowe, Hereditary Grand Whipping-Boy to the Royal House of England. And do not worry. I will take up my studies again and do so badly that the Royal Treasurer will have to triple your salary."

"Rise, Hereditary Grand Whipping-Boy."

THE PRINCE AND THE PAUPER

Tom then realized that the grateful boy could be of help to him, for he was full of facts about court people and court matters. Young Marlowe was delighted to visit often and chat, believing he was helping cure his beloved king and restore his memory.

So instructive were these conversations that when Lord Hertford came to coach Tom on how to act when he would be dining at a state dinner in public in four days, Tom needed very little help. Humphrey had covered it all.

Lord Hertford, seeing this "improved memory," decided to press the king a bit further. "Can Your Majesty tax your memory just a bit more, and tell me where the late king's Great Royal Seal is?"

Tom looked up blankly. "The Great Royal Seal? What does it look like, my Lord?"

Hertford feared he had pushed the boy too far—the king had lost his wits again! "No matter, Sire," he said. "Let us speak of more important things."

"Where Is the Great Royal Seal?"

"I Wonder What That's All About."

CHAPTER 9

Tom Dispenses Justice

Tom had grown somewhat more comfortable in his kingly duties, and while waiting to receive some court officials, he wandered over to the window of the large audience room. He was surprised to see an unruly mob of the lowest and poorest class on the road leading to the palace.

"I wonder what that's all about," he said.

No sooner were the words out than Hertford sent a page to the captain of the guard with an order to halt the mob and ask the reason they were there.

In a few moments, the messenger returned.

THE PRINCE AND THE PAUPER

"The crowd, Your Majesty, is following a man, a woman, and a young girl."

"Following them? Why?" asked Tom.

"The three are on their way to being executed for crimes against our kingdom."

With no thought at all for the broken laws or the suffering victims of their crime, Tom felt a wave of pity for the three prisoners. "Have them brought here!" he ordered.

The page bowed and left.

At that moment, the expected titled guests were announced and began to fill the room. But Tom hardly noticed them as he sat waiting in the Chair of State.

In a little while, the tramping feet of the king's guards were heard. The men entered with a sheriff and the three accused. As the group knelt, Tom felt his memory stir at the sight of one of the prisoners.

"I *know* that man," he told himself. "I saw him on New Year's Day at ten o'clock. I'm sure of the time, because the clock was striking

"Have Them Brought Here!"

eleven about an hour later when Gammer Canty gave me the beating of my life. . . . I'll never forget that stranger. He fished my friend, Giles Witt, out of the Thames that bitter windy day, and saved his life."

But all he said aloud was, "Remove the woman and girl to the next room. I wish to know more about this man's offense."

"Your Majesty, he killed a man by poisoning him," explained the sheriff.

"And has that been proved?"

"Most clearly, Sire."

The stranger clasped his hands. "Your Grace!" he cried. "I beg your mercy. I am innocent, and the proof was weak, but let that go. All I ask now is that you take pity and order me *hanged!*"

"What?" said Tom. "Won't that happen to you anyway?"

"Oh, no, Your Majesty. I am to be boiled alive!"

Tom turned to Hertford. "Can this be true?"

The Prisoner Begs for Mercy.

"It is the law for poisoners, Your Grace. But it is better than in Germany, where the criminal is lowered slowly by a rope so that first his feet, then his legs —"

"Enough! I order that law changed at once. No one else must die such a hideous death!"

The sheriff was about to remove the man when Tom spoke again. "One moment. The man said the proof was weak. What was the proof, sheriff?"

"The prisoner visited the sick man's house in Islington town. Three witnesses saw him enter and leave. An hour later, the man died, his muscles twitching fiercely."

"Did anybody see him give the poison? Was any found?"

"No, Your Grace, but the doctor testified that this kind of death comes only from poisoning. And there's something else. Many people testified that a witch, who since left town, had *foretold* that the sick man would die of poison given by a stranger."

"What Was the Proof, Sheriff?"

"It looks pretty bad for you," Tom said to the man. "Do you have anything to say on your behalf?"

"Nothing, Your Majesty. I have no friends, or I would show that at the very moment they say I was *taking* a life, I was actually far from there, *saving* one."

"Peace!" cried Tom. "Sheriff, when was the deed done?"

"At ten in the morning on the first day of the year, Your —"

"Free the prisoner! It is the king's will. I will not have a man hanged on such harebrained evidence!"

The room began to buzz with admiration for the king's spirit and wisdom, and with joy that the king's wits had returned. Tom enjoyed the applause, but it also aroused his curiosity more. He ordered the woman and girl brought forth.

"What have they done?" he asked the sheriff.

"Free the Prisoner!"

"Sold themselves to the Devil," said the sheriff. "A crime punishable by hanging."

"Where and when was this done?" asked Tom.

"It was on a midnight in December, in a ruined church, Sire."

"Who was there at the time?"

"Only these two and the Devil."

"Have they confessed?"

"No, Your Grace. They deny it."

"If no one else was there and they have not confessed, then how did the crime get known?"

"Witnesses saw them heading there. What's more, they used their powers to cause a terrible storm that ruined the whole area. About forty witnesses who suffered from the storm swore to that."

"And did this woman also suffer as a result of the storm?"

"Yes, Your Majesty. And well she *deserved* to have her house swept away."

The Sheriff Accuses a Woman and a Girl.

"She would have to be mad to ruin her own home and leave herself and child without shelter," announced Tom. "And if she's mad, she didn't know what she was doing, and therefore, she isn't guilty."

Heads nodded, and one elderly nobleman whispered to another, "If this king is mad himself, then it is a madness that should be caught by many sane people."

"By the way," Tom asked the sheriff, "how did they cause the storm?"

"By pulling off their stockings, Sire."

The answer astonished Tom and also made him curious. "Why, that's wonderful!" he cried. Then, turning to the woman, he said, "Please—use your power and show me a storm."

The superstitious people in the room turned pale and trembled. The woman prisoner looked astonished.

"Do not be afraid," continued Tom. "You will not be blamed. In fact, if you make just a tiny

Nobles Admire Tom's Decisions.

bit of thunder, you will be pardoned, and you and your child will walk out free."

The woman sank to the ground in tears. "Tour Majesty," she cried. "I have no such power. I would gladly do it if I could—to save my child's life."

"I believe her," Tom told the assemblage. "If my mother were in her place, she would do it in a minute if she could, to save me. So would any mother." Then to the woman, he said, "You are free, good woman, and your child too. But now that it is all over, do pull off your stockings. Produce a storm and you will be rich."

The woman obeyed. But though she pulled off both her stockings and the child's as well, no storm followed.

"All right, good woman," said Tom. "No more proof is necessary. Your power has left. But if it ever returns, do not forget my orders. Come back here and make me a storm."

Tom's justice brought many noble smiles.

"No More Proof Is Necessary."

Miles Guards the Doorway.

CHAPTER 10

Foo-Foo, King of the Mooncalves

Meanwhile, Edward Tudor was making himself comfortable in Miles Hendon's only bed. At his host's questioning look, Edward ordered, "You will sleep across the doorway and guard it."

Miles, accustomed to sleeping in worse places, smiled in admiration. "Truly, he should have been born a king," he said as he stretched out on the floor.

The next morning, Miles thought to surprise the ragged boy. After measuring the sleeping form with some string, he dashed out, returning a short while later with a suit of used but clean clothing. But the boy was gone!

THE PRINCE AND THE PAUPER

"Innkeeper! Innkeeper!" he shouted.

A servant came in with the breakfast tray, and Miles sprang at him. "Tell me fast or you're a dead man—where's the boy?"

Trembling, the servant explained, "When-when your worship left, a tall, heavy youth ran up and said you wanted to see the boy at the Southwark end of the bridge right away. The boy grumbled a bit, but went with him."

"Oh, no! Think now. Were they alone?"

"Only at first. Then a rough-looking man jumped out of the crowd and joined them."

"Out of my way, idiot!" Miles cried, and he plunged down the stairs two at a time.

After a futile search on the bridge and throughout Southwark, Miles rested at an inn and tried to reason things out. "It must have been that scurvy villain who claimed to be the boy's father. But knowing the poor, mad lad, he'd probably try to escape. But where to? Since I'm his only friend, he'd most likely look for me. He knew I was heading home to

"Where's the Boy?"

Hendon Hall. *That's* where I must get to right away."

When Edward and the heavy young man reached the Southwark end of the bridge, the rough man who was waiting did not join them, but limped along behind. A green patch covered one eye, his arm was in a sling, and he walked with the help of an oaken staff.

After a long walk through Southwark, the three reached a highway.

Annoyed now, Edward cried, "Enough! Let Hendon come to *me!*"

"You'll wait here while your friend lies wounded?" asked the youth.

"*Wounded?* Lead on, and faster!"

When they reached a forest, the youth picked out a trail of sticks in the ground with little rags on them. He followed that trail until they reached a clearing with the burnt-out remains of an old barn. The youth entered, and Edward followed eagerly.

"Where is he?" Edward asked, seeing no one

Following a Trail of Sticks

and now becoming suspicious.

A mocking laugh was the answer. Enraged, the king grabbed a chunk of wood and was about to strike when another laugh rang out. It was the lame ruffian who had been following them.

"Who are you?" demanded Edward.

"Is my disguise so good, you don't know your own old man?" growled John Canty.

"You are not my father. I am the king. And if you've hidden my servant Miles —"

"I see you're still crazy, so I won't punish you—unless you make trouble! Get this straight now—I'm wanted for murder, so keep your mouth shut! Now, where are your mother and sisters? They didn't meet me at the bridge."

"My mother is dead, and my sister is in the palace."

The heavy young man burst into mocking laughter and lunged at the boy.

"Don't bother with him, Hugo," said Canty.

"I'm Wanted for Murder!"

THE PRINCE AND THE PAUPER

"He's mad. Let him go on with his ravings."

As the two whispered together in a dark corner of the barn, the tired king drew back to another corner and after a time of quiet thinking about his dead father, fell asleep in the straw.

He awoke to the sound of coarse laughter. Lifting his head, he saw a fire at the other end of the barn. Around it sprawled a scary crew—big long-haired men in rags, blind beggars with bandaged eyes, crippled beggars with wooden legs, and women—from half-grown girls to wrinkled hags—who were loud and dirty. Plus there were a couple of sore-faced babies and some half-starved dogs to lead the blind.

"Pass that whiskey!" somebody yelled. "And let's have a song!"

At this call, one of the "blind" men stood up. He pulled the patches from his healthy eyes and threw aside his "Help the Blind" sign.

Another beggar unfastened the wooden leg

A Scary Crew!

from around his perfect one, and a lively song and dance followed.

When it was over, the thieves and beggars gathered round John Canty and greeted him like an old friend.

"What've you been up to lately?" asked one.

"Killed a man. A priest," said Canty.

This news brought cheers and applause.

"How many in our gang now, Ruffler?" Canty asked the leader.

"Some twenty-five. Most are here. The rest are heading east. We follow at dawn. We've also got some new men." Then he shouted, "Step up, Hodge and Burns. You too, Yokel. Show your decorations."

All had rope welts on their backs. Burns lifted his hair to show where his left ear had once been, and Hodge pointed to a "V" branded into his shoulder. Then Yokel spoke.

"I used to be a farmer with a nice family. That's over now. They took my land to turn into sheep ranges. My wife and I had to beg for

The New Men Show Their Decorations.

food for our kids. That's against the law, so they whipped us, and she died. Drink to my poor kids, who never harmed anyone, but they starved to death anyway while I got hunted down. And here on my cheek, if I washed the stain off, you'd see an "S". Yes, I'm a slave, a runaway. And if they find me, curse the English law, I'll hang!"

A voice came ringing through the hazy air. "No, you will not! From this day on, that law is ended!"

Everybody turned as the little king strode forward. "Who are you?" they asked.

"I am Edward, King of England," he said with dignity.

The crowd broke into wild laughter, and Canty had to struggle to make himself heard. "That's my loony son," he said. "The crazy dreamer really thinks he's the king."

"I *am* the king," protested Edward, "as you will find out in good time. You have confessed a murder, and you will hang for it."

"That's My Loony Son."

THE PRINCE AND THE PAUPER

"What?" roared Canty. "You'd turn me in? Just let me get my hands on you —"

The Ruffler knocked him down with one punch. "Have you no respect for kings or Rufflers?" Then he turned to Edward. "Make no more threats against any of my mates, nor say anything bad about them on the outside. You can play at being a king if you want, but don't really calf yourself King Edward. That's *treason*. We may be bad in some ways, but we're no traitors. Watch this, for proof. All together now. 'Long live Edward, King of England!' "

"LONG LIVE EDWARD, KING OF ENGLAND!" came the hearty response.

The little king's face lighted with pleasure as he said simply, "I thank you, good people."

Again the company roared with laughter. When they quieted down a bit, Ruffler said to Edward, firmly but with good nature, "Drop it, I said. Imagine whatever you want, but pick some other title."

The Ruffler Scolds Edward.

THE PRINCE AND THE PAUPER

A tinker—a pot-mender—shouted, "Let's call him Foo-Foo the First, King of the Mooncalves!"

An answering shout went up. "Long live Foo-Foo, King of the Mooncalves!"

"Crown him!"

"Robe him!"

"Scepter him!"

"Throne him!"

Before he knew what was happening, Edward was crowned with a basin, robed in a tattered blanket, throned on a barrel, and sceptered with a tinker's soldering iron. All around him the crowd knelt and pretended to be begging favors.

"Pity us, your slaves, and honor us with a royal kick, oh noble Foo-Foo!"

"Spit upon us please, that we may brag of it to our children."

Tears of shame and anger filled the eyes of the little king. "I offered them kindness and they return it with cruelty," he sobbed.

"Long Live Foo-Foo!"

Hugo Goes Into His Act.

CHAPTER 11

The King on the Run

Ruffler's band started out on their thieving at early dawn. Edward's one thought was to escape as he was sent off in Hugo's care to either steal or beg. When Edward refused, Hugo ordered him to act as his decoy.

Soon, a kind-looking stranger approached them on the road, and Hugo went into his act. He rolled his eyes, groaned, tottered around, and collapsed at the stranger's feet, writhing in seeming agony.

"Oh, dear!" cried the stranger. "You poor soul. Let me help you up."

"No, no, good sir," gasped Hugo. "It hurts me

to be touched when I am like this. My brother here will tell you of my pain when these fits come on. A penny please, sir. A penny for a little food."

"A penny? I'll give you three, poor boy." And he took them from his pocket. Then he called to Edward, "Come here, son, and help me carry your sick brother over to —"

"I'm *not* his brother," interrupted the king. "He's a beggar and a thief. He's got the money you just gave him, and he's picked your pocket too. He's not really sick, but if you want to cure him, hit him with your stick!"

But Hugo didn't wait to be cured. He was off like the wind, with the stranger in pursuit.

Grateful that he was at last free, the king fled in the other direction—into a dense forest. He did not slow down till nightfall. At last he saw a glimmer of light. He made for it and found himself before a simple hut. Through the open window he heard a voice in prayer. Standing on tiptoe, he saw a large, bony man

"He's a Beggar and a Thief!"

with snowy white hair and whiskers, praying before a candlelit shrine. His long robe was of sheepskins, and beside him on an old wooden box lay a thick book and a human skull.

"A holy hermit," said Edward, and he thought it safe to knock on the man's door.

When the man called out for him to enter, Edward did so, explaining, "I am the king."

"Oh, welcome then!" cried the hermit with enthusiasm. "It is a joy to see somebody of high position in rags. You have given up all your riches for a simple holy life. Well, here your soul will surely become pure. You will wear rough clothing, pray most of time, eat only crusts and herbs, and whip your body daily."

The startled king tried to speak, but the hermit went right on.

"Sh! I will tell you a secret. I was supposed to be pope, but the king broke up my religious house and I, a poor monk, was sent homeless

A Holy Hermit

into the world. That's when a group of angels came to me and made me an archangel instead!"

The old hermit went on in his frenzy for an hour, while Edward sat and suffered. Then the man's voice softened, and his gentleness won the king's heart completely.

After making Edward comfortable before a fire, the old man made supper for the two of them and doctored the boy's bruises. Then he tucked him snugly and lovingly into a bed in one corner of the room.

As he straightened up, he asked, "You say you're the king?"

"Yes," came the sleepy reply

"Of what country?"

"England, of course."

"England? Then Henry's dead?"

"Yes, sadly. I am his son."

At this, the hermit clenched his fists and frowned. "Do you know that he's the one who made me homeless?"

The Hermit Tells His Story.

THE PRINCE AND THE PAUPER

There was no answer. The old man bent over the sleeping boy, and a look of evil satisfaction replaced his frown. Mumbling to himself, he began searching about the house till he found what he wanted—a rusty old butcher knife and a sharpening stone. Then he sat down by the fire and busied himself sharpening the blade, all the while muttering and chuckling to himself.

"It's all his father's doing. I'm only an archangel because King Henry kept me from being what my dream foretold—the pope!"

Noiselessly moving about the hut, he gathered some rags and leather strips. Then he returned to the bed and tied the boy's ankles and wrists. Around his head he wound and knotted a bandage, doing it all so gently that the boy didn't stir.

The hermit went back to the fire and sat watching the slumbering boy. He resembled a monstrous spider gloating over a helpless insect in his web.

Tying the Boy's Ankles and Wrists

THE PRINCE AND THE PAUPER

At last, Edward's eyes opened, and he lay staring in frozen horror at the knife.

The old man's evil smile was fixed as he cried out, "Son of Henry the Eighth, say the prayer for the dying!"

The boy struggled helplessly to free himself as tears rolled down his face. The old man leaned over the bed and sank down to his knees. Raising the knife, he brought it towards the struggling boy.

Suddenly, noises outside the cabin interrupted the hermit's rambled mutterings, and he dropped the knife. Then came the sound of running feet and angry voices, and a pounding on the door.

"Open up, and hurry!" The voice was the most blessed sound to the king's ears, for it was Miles Hendon's.

The enraged hermit moved swiftly to open the door, then closed it behind him. Edward heard Hendon explain that he had caught the kidnappers and they had confessed following

"Say the Prayer for the Dying!"

the boy to the hut.

"Now where is he?" demanded Hendon.

"I have sent him on an errand," said the hermit.

"Show me the direction he took; he may be lost in the woods."

Bound and unable to make a sound, the desperate boy heard their voices fade. He waited in terror, dreading the hermit's return. Some minutes later, he heard the door open. The sound chilled him to his bones, and he closed his eyes in horror.

When he dared to open them again, his horror returned, for before him stood John Canty and Hugo! In minutes he was freed and being rushed through the forest by his two new captors.

And so he was back again with the outlaw gang, befriended by most of them, but taunted by Canty and Hugo behind Ruffler's back. Twice Hugo "accidentally" stepped on Edward's toes, and twice the king ignored it.

"I Have Sent Him on an Errand."

But the third time he lost his temper and attacked the bully. Picking up a stout stick, he knocked Hugo down.

Hugo, furious, grabbed a stick too and came at his small opponent. A ring formed around them, betting and yelling and cheering. Though Hugo moved his bulk frantically, he was no match for the well-trained king, who had been taught swordsmanship by Europe's masters.

Edward caught and returned every blow neatly, moving like lightning into every opening.

Soon Hugo, bruised and mocked, slunk from the field, while the king was carried on the shoulders of the joyous rabble to the place of honor beside the Ruffler.

"From now on," said the leader, "anyone who calls him Foo-Foo is banished. We will now crown him our King of the Game-Cocks!"

"All hail the King of the Game-Cocks!"

Edward Knocks Hugo Down.

Applying a *Clime* to Edward's Leg

CHAPTER 12

A Surprise at Hendon Hall

Hugo was not a good loser. He made two plans for getting revenge against the little fighter who had beaten him, but was still in his care when he went out begging. First, to shame Edward's proud spirit, he had a *clime* put on the boy's leg—a purposely-made sore that was supposed to win the pity of strangers and make them generous to the "poor diseased beggar."

Hugo, with the tinker's help, made a paste of strong lime, soap and iron rust, and applied it to a strip of leather, which was tied tightly to the boy's leg. This would eat away the skin.

Edward struggled, but the two held him down as the paste burned into his skin. Luckily, before the job was completed, Yokel, the farmer, came upon them. He ripped off the leather strip and marched the three up to the Ruffler.

"No more!" said the leader. "He shall not beg for us. The boy deserves something better than begging. From now on, I'm promoting him to stealing!"

This played right into Hugo's second plan, which was to get the boy blamed for a crime and then to betray him to the law.

That afternoon, Hugo dragged Edward to a neighboring village, Hugo looking for a victim and Edward looking for a chance to escape. Hugo's chance, however, came first.

A woman came by with a large package in a basket. Hugo crept up behind her, grabbed the package, and ran back to Edward, pulling an old piece of blanket from his pocket and wrapping it around the package.

Hugo Steals a Package.

THE PRINCE AND THE PAUPER

The woman didn't see Hugo's action, but felt her basket grow lighter. When she began to scream that she'd been robbed, Hugo thrust the package into Edward's hands and fled down a crooked alley.

The king, highly insulted, threw the bundle on the ground. The blanket fell away, exposing the stolen goods. The woman quickly seized his wrist with one hand and began calling for help to the crowd that began to close around them.

"Let's teach this young thief a lesson!" someone shouted.

Just then, a sword flashed in the air and the familiar, welcome voice said, "Unhand the boy, madam. Let the law handle this."

The king sprang to his rescuer's side, exclaiming, "Sir Miles. Now carve this mob to ribbons for me!"

Smiling, Hendon whispered to the boy, "Do not speak so, My Prince. Just trust me; all will end up well." Then to himself he added, *"Sir*

The Woman Seizes Edward's Wrist.

Miles! I had forgotten that I was knighted by the King of Dreams and Shadows."

Moments later, a constable of the law arrived and was about to reach for Edward when Hendon said, "That won't be necessary. I guarantee that he'll go peacefully."

As the officer led the way, Miles whispered to the king, "Do not think of running off. That would be breaking the law. When you are back on your throne, you will remember that you once had respect for your own laws."

Edward nodded. "You are right. Whatever laws my subjects must obey, I will too, while I am dressed as one."

When they all stood before the judge, the woman swore that Edward was the one who had taken her bundle, which turned out to have a plump dressed pig in it.

"How much is it worth?" asked the judge.

"Thirty-eight pence, Your Worship," said the woman.

"Hmm. Clear the crowd from the court and

Miles Steps In.

close the doors," he ordered. "Only the boy, the woman, the constable, and Hendon are to stay."

That done, the judge explained the law. "Anyone convicted of stealing something that costs more than thirteen pence is to be hanged."

Miles and the king grew pale until the woman spoke. "Please change its value to eight pence, then. I wouldn't want to cause the death of this hungry lad."

As the judge nodded and began to write in his record book, Miles surprised the king by throwing his arms around the boy and hugging him. Then the woman took her bundle and headed for the door. To Miles' surprise, the constable followed her. Curious to know why, he slipped out into the hall and hid in the shadows to hear their conversation.

"That's a fine pig," said the constable. "I'll buy it from you for eight pence."

"Are you crazy?" cried the woman. "I paid

The Judge Explains the Law.

thirty-eight pence for it. Eight pence, huh!"

"Is that so? Then you swore under oath in there falsely! All I have to do now is go back and report it. You'll get arrested and the boy will hang!"

"Oh, here then. Give me the eight pence and keep quiet." And the woman went off crying.

Hendon slipped back into the courtroom. The constable hid his prize and followed.

The judge was saying to the boy, " . . . to be spent in jail, to teach you not to take what isn't yours. Also a public beating. Constable, take him away."

Hendon's look stopped the king from crying out, and he took Edward's hand to lead him outside.

Once in the street, Edward pulled his hand away and stopped. "Do you expect *me* to enter a common jail?" he cried.

"*Please* trust me," whispered Miles.

When they reached a deserted square, Miles turned to the constable. "Just turn your back

"You'll Get Arrested!"

now, and let the boy escape," he whispered.

"What! Now, I'll arrest *you* for —"

"Don't be so hasty, my man," said Miles. "The pig you bought for eight pence might cost you your life."

"Oh that? That was just a little joke."

"Good. Then wait here a minute while I go back and share a laugh with the judge." And he prepared to head back to the court.

"No, no!" cried the constable. "The judge has no sense of humor. He'll have me —. Never mind. I'll turn my back."

"Fine. And you are to return the pig to the woman."

"That I will, and I'll never touch another. I'll just say that you broke in and took the prisoner from me by force. I'll smash the door myself."

"Do it then," said Miles. "And do not worry. The judge had kind feelings toward the boy, and he won't be hard on you for letting him escape."

"You Are To Return the Pig."

THE PRINCE AND THE PAUPER

Once the constable was gone, Miles took Edward back to his inn and dressed him in the suit of used clothes he had bought for the boy. Then they set off for Hendon Hall on Miles' old donkeys.

As they rode, they told of their adventures while they were apart. Then, Miles spoke of his kind father, his generous brother Arthur, and of the lovely Edith. He even managed a brotherly comment about Hugh. How happy they all would be to see him!

On the last day of the trip, Miles called out, "There it is!" And he pointed excitedly. "See the towers, and my father's park. Know how many rooms we have? *Seventy,* and also *twenty servants.* Not bad, eh?"

They turned onto a narrow road which led to the stately mansion. Hendon sprang to the ground and helped the king down. Then, taking the boy by the hand, he rushed through the great door and into a large hallway.

In a room to one side, a thin, balding man

Arriving at Hendon Hall

sat writing at a carved table near the fire-place. "Your brother's home, Hugh!" cried Miles, holding out his arms. "Come greet me, and call our father!"

Hugh looked surprised for a split-second, then his expression grew puzzled. "I'm afraid you're mad, poor stranger," he said softly. "As your clothing shows, you've probably gone through rough times."

"Poor stranger? Come, Hugh. Don't you know your own brother?"

Hugh pulled Miles to the window and studied him from head to foot. Finally, he shook his head sadly. "No," he said. "I wish it were so—that I did recognize you as my brother. But I fear that the letter which came six years ago was right. My brother died in battle."

"That's a lie!" protested Miles. "Just call our father. He'll know me."

"I cannot call the dead."

"Father is dead?" Miles said, trembling.

"Your Brother's Home, Hugh!"

"My joy at being home is gone. Then, please, call my brother Arthur. He will know me."

"He's dead too."

"Oh, no! Please don't tell me Lady Edith—"

"Is dead? No, she is alive."

"Thank God for that. Bring her, then, and any of the old servants too."

In a little while, a beautiful, dark-haired lady, richly clothed in velvet, entered after Hugh. They were followed by five servants.

Hendon sprang forward. "Oh, Edith, my darling—"

Hugh waved him back. "Look him over," he said to the lady. "Do you recognize him?"

The woman trembled and her cheeks flushed. Slowly she lifted her head and looked at him with frightened eyes. "I do not know him," she said in a dead voice. And covering a sob, she fled from the room.

Then Hugh turned to the servants. "Do you know him?" he asked.

All of them shook their heads.

"I Do Not Know Him."

"You see," said Hugh. "There must be some mistake. The servants didn't recognize you, nor did my wife."

"Your *wife!*" gasped Miles, and in an instant he had pinned his brother to the wall with an iron grip about his throat. "*Now* I understand. *You* wrote the letter saying I was dead so you could steal both my bride and my property. You had better leave now, or I'll shame my soldier's honor by killing a miserable little man!"

Hugh, almost suffocated, collapsed into a chair. "Grab him and tie him up!" he shouted.

The servants hesitated. "He's armed," said one.

"Then go get weapons, cowards, while I send for help." With that, he headed for the door, where he turned and said to Miles, "You had better not try to escape."

"Escape? Have no fear of that. Miles Hendon is master of Hendon Hall and all that it contains. He will stay all right."

Miles Pins His Brother to the Wall.

Edward is Puzzled.

CHAPTER 13

Trial and Punishment

"It is very strange," said Edward when they were alone. "I just cannot explain it."

"Nothing strange at all, My Lord. My brother has always been dishonest."

"No, not that," said Edward. "I mean that the king isn't missed. Why aren't messengers being sent around describing me and looking for me? Shouldn't it cause concern when the head of a nation disappears?"

"Oh, yes, that's true," said Miles. But to himself he added, "Poor little madman, poor little Ruler of Dreams and Shadows."

"Listen to my plan, though," cried Edward

excitedly. "I will write out a letter at this desk here, in three languages—Latin, Greek, and English. If you just get it to my uncle, Lord Hertford, he will know I wrote it."

Miles let the boy do as he wanted; his mind was elsewhere. So when Edward finally handed Miles the paper, he absent-mindedly put it in his pocket and spoke of what was on his mind—Lady Edith's behavior.

"How oddly she acted. She seemed to know me, but she *said* she didn't. Yet my Edith wouldn't lie, unless—that's it! He *forced* her to lie, and she feared to tell the truth in front of him. I'll go find her now and —"

Just then the door opened and Lady Edith entered, pale and sad, but with grace and dignity.

"I've come to warn you," she said. "You are in great danger. Hugh is an evil and powerful man, and I am forced to be a slave to him. If you didn't resemble Miles Hendon, Hugh would simply denounce you as a madman and

"I Will Write Out a Letter."

an impostor and everyone would agree. But you *do* resemble Miles, and if Hugh realized it, he would destroy you. He is a tyrant, and you have threatened him in his own house. Take this purse, I beg you, and bribe the servants to let you go."

"Thank you, no. But tell me one thing. *Am* I Miles Hendon?"

"No," she said nervously. "I do not know you. Now hurry and save yourself!"

At that moment, officers burst into the room and, after a struggle, put Hendon and the boy in chains and led them off to prison.

They spent troubled days and nights in a cell with twenty rowdy jailmates whose noisy singing and brawling kept them awake until the jailer clubbed a couple of heads.

After a week of this, the jailer appeared with an old man. "The villain's in this cell," he told the visitor. "See if you can tell which one he is."

Miles recognized the man as an old Hendon

"Hurry and Save Yourself!"

family servant. "Blake Andrews will know me," he said to himself, "but he will probably deny it like the rest of them."

Sure enough, the old man looked around and said, "Miles Hendon isn't here. Which one claims to be him?"

The jailer laughed. "Check this big animal," he said, pointing to Miles.

The servant approached him, looked him over, then shook his head. "This is not Hendon," he said.

The jailer laughed again and sauntered off, leaving the old man to amuse himself by cursing the impostor. But instead, the old man dropped to his knees and whispered, "Thank God you're back, Master Hendon. I believed you were dead all these years. I'm old and poor, but just say the word and I'll tell the truth, even if they hang me."

"No, you mustn't. It wouldn't help either of us. But thank you for giving me back my faith in man."

In a Noisy, Crowded Cell

THE PRINCE AND THE PAUPER

In the next few days, old Blake Andrews came often, supposedly to amuse himself at that phony Hendon's expense. But actually, he smuggled decent food to Miles and the boy and, in between his loud insults, whispered news of the outside world.

That is how Edward learned that in just one week, on February 20th, the new king would be crowned at Westminster Abbey, and that Hugh Hendon would be going to that ceremony in the hopes of being named a lord by a friend at court, the Lord Protector.

"What Lord Protector?" asked Edward.

"The Duke of Somerset," answered Andrews.

"Who is the Duke of Somerset?"

"Why, the Earl of Hertford, of course."

"Oh? And who made him a duke and the Lord Protector?"

"The king, of course!"

The boy started violently. "*What* king?" he shouted.

Blake Andrews Smuggles In Food.

THE PRINCE AND THE PAUPER

"Why, His Sacred Majesty, King Edward the Sixth. There are some who say he's mad, but if he is, he's getting better daily. He has begun his reign most kindly too, by pardoning the Duke of Norfolk and by changing some of England's cruelest laws."

The king was struck dumb in amazement. "Is it possible," he wondered, "that the little beggar boy I left dressed in my clothes has taken the throne?" The mystery perplexed the boy and made him more impatient than ever to escape.

The harshness of prison life took all of Edward's attention for a while. He saw first hand the unfairness of the law. Two women who had befriended him were burned at the stake because of their religious beliefs, before the eyes of their daughters shrieking in horror and before the eyes of the little king, who swore that the scene would stay with him all his life.

Edward also learned that another woman

Burning at the Stake!

would be hanged for stealing a yard of cloth, and a man for killing a deer in the king's park.

An old lawyer who had written a pamphlet against the Lord Chancellor would have his ears cut off, his cheeks branded, and be imprisoned for life.

The boy was enraged over these inhumanities and swore to himself: "When I return to my throne, I will see to it these shameful laws are swept off the books."

Finally the time came for Miles Hendon's trial. He was accused of attacking Hugh - Hendon in his home, but no one mentioned his claim that he was Miles Hendon. And he was sentenced to sit for two hours in the public stocks. Because of his youth, Edward was let off with a warning to avoid such bad company.

When the king saw his faithful servant and friend locked into place on the platform amid the jeering crowd, he was furious. Then someone let fly an egg that landed on Miles' face, and the king could no longer control his

An Egg Lands on Miles' Face.

temper. "Let him go!" he cried. "I am the —"

"Give that brat a couple of lashes," called an officer, "to teach him a lesson."

"Better make that six," said Hugh Hendon, who had ridden up to watch Miles' punishment.

The king clenched his teeth as two officers seized him. He had to either take the punishment or try to get out of it by pleading for mercy. He chose the whipping—a king could not beg.

But Miles spoke up. "Let the child go. I will take his lashes."

"Splendid!" said Hugh with an evil laugh. "Let the little beggar go and give this fellow a dozen in his place. Well laid on too!"

Miles was removed from the stocks and his bare back severely whipped. Edward watched, tears streaming down his cheeks, as Miles took the lashes without a sound.

Finally, when Miles was returned to the stocks, the king stepped up to him and

"Give That Brat a Couple of Lashes!"

whispered, "I will *never* forget your noble conduct on the king's behalf."

Edward then picked up the whip from the ground and gently touched Hendon's bleeding shoulder with it. "Edward of England dubs you Earl!" he said.

Despite his pain, Miles was touched, and his eyes filled with tears. "Poor lad," he muttered. "First I was a knight in his Kingdom of Dreams and Shadows, and now I am his make-believe earl. But he gives the title in love and I shall take it in love."

When his time in the stocks was up, Miles was ordered to leave the area and never return.

At first, the good soldier had no idea of where to go. Then, remembering what old Andrews had said about the young king's fairness, he decided to strike for London. Perhaps his father's old friend, Sir Humphrey Marlowe, could help him get an audience with the new ruler.

He wondered how the boy would feel about

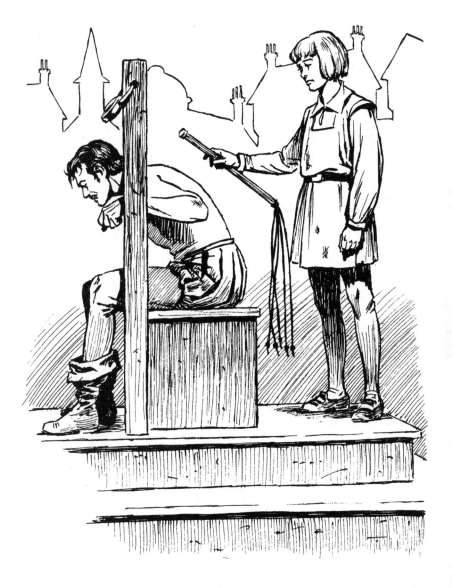

"Edward of England Dubs You Earl."

returning to the place where he had known only misery, so continuing his role of servant, he asked, "Where to, My Lord?"

"To London!" came the surprising reply.

At about ten o'clock on the night of February 19th, the two reached London Bridge, to find everybody full of drink in early celebration of the following day's coronation.

A few rotting heads of noblemen punished by King Henry for various crimes still decorated the upright spears of the bridge. One of these heads now fell and hit Hendon's arm before it landed on the ground. A beer-jolly citizen stumbled over it and fell against somebody else. He, in turn, hit the first person he could reach, and was knocked out by that man's friend.

The free-for-all that followed soon became a riot, and Miles Hendon and Edward Tudor were hopelessly separated.

Lost Among Celebrating Crowds!

Enjoying His Royal Life

CHAPTER 14

The Great Seal Test

By now, Tom Canty was thoroughly enjoying his royal life and thinking less and less of the real prince who had vanished. When Tom wanted to talk, he would send for Princess Elizabeth and Lady Jane. He came to enjoy being dressed ceremoniously, marching to dinner in a procession, and receiving great ambassadors. But he remained kind-hearted and fair as he changed unjust laws.

Midnight of February 19th found Tom Canty drifting to sleep in his rich bed guarded by his loyal servants. That same midnight found Edward, the true king, hungry, tired, and dirty, wedged in with a crowd outside Westminster Abbey, watching the busy workmen making last-minute preparations for the next day's coronation.

On the morning of the 20th, Tom, splendidly dressed and on a white horse with rich trappings, led an almost endless procession.

He smiled and waved to the thousands who lined the way, cheering. Every now and then he would fling a handful of bright coins to the scrambling pack.

At one point, as he was about to throw out another handful, he caught sight of a pale, astonished face in the crowd, its eyes fixed on him. His hand, palm outward, flew up before his eyes—his old habit—as he recognized his mother.

The next instant, the woman had torn her way past the guards and was hugging and kissing his leg. "Oh, my child, my darling!" she cried, her face full of joy and love.

The guard snatched her back and pushed her

Tom Leads the Procession.

into the crowd just as the words, "I do not know you, woman!" fell from Tom's lips.

But her broken-hearted expression shamed Tom. His heart was eaten with sorrow and all he could think of was, "I wish to God I were free of my imprisonment."

He no longer flung the coins, but rode with bowed head and empty eyes as his conscience kept repeating those shameful words: *I do not know you, woman!*

When the crowd began to notice the king's changed attitude, the Lord Protector became worried. He rode up to the king, saying, "Shake off that sad expression, Sire. The eyes of England are on you. . . . It was that crazy beggar-woman that disturbed Your Highness. I'll have her —"

Tom turned and, in a numb voice, said, "She was my mother."

"My God!" groaned the Lord Protector. "The old madness is upon him again!"

The procession reached the Abbey. That

"I Do Not Know You, Woman!"

great building was filled with dukes, earls, barons, and ladies in jewels.

At the center of the platform and raised up four steps stood the throne. On its seat was a rough, flat rock, the Stone of Scone, on which Scottish kings once sat to be crowned. Today, the throne and footstool were covered with cloth-of-gold.

The great heads of the church and the Archbishop of Canterbury mounted the platform. A peal of music burst forth, and Tom Canty, in a golden robe, was led to the throne. Pale and despondent, the boy felt only regret.

The Archbishop lifted the heavy crown from its cushion and held it over Tom's head. Every nobleman raised his own diamond coronet above his own head, and sparkling flashes filled the great church.

At this impressive moment, an unexpected figure moved down the center aisle—a bareheaded, ragged boy. "I forbid you to set the crown upon that head!" he cried. "*I* am the

Crowning the King

king! I am Edward Tudor!"

In an instant, several angry hands grabbed the boy, but in the same instant, Tom Canty stepped forward and, in a ringing voice, called out, "Let him go! He *is* the king!"

Everyone froze except Hertford, who exclaimed, "Do not mind His Majesty! His sickness is upon him again! Seize the boy!"

But those ready to obey were stopped when Tom stamped his foot and cried, "Do not dare touch him! He is the king!"

Lords and ladies looked at each other in confusion. No one moved except the ragged boy as he made his way to the platform.

Tom quickly ran to him and fell to his knees. "Your Majesty," he cried, "let poor Tom Canty be the first to swear loyalty to Your Honored Self. Put on the crown and take over what is rightly yours."

But Hertford, who recognized the strong resemblance between the two boys, was not convinced. "If it please Your Majesty, I wish to

"I am Edward Tudor!"

ask some questions first," he said. "And remember, a false claim is *serious.* Two kings,
could divide the land in war. We must arrest a
traitorous pretender."

Edward answered all he was asked about
the royal family and the palace, so many now
believed him. But the Lord Protector still had
doubts. "Anyone could learn those facts," he
said. "No, arrest—but wait!"

Hertford's face suddenly lit up. "I have the
perfect test." Then turning to the ragged boy,
he said, "If you can tell us the one thing our
king cannot, the throne is yours. Where is the
Great Seal of England?"

Edward turned to one of the noblemen,
commanding, "My Lord St. John, go to my cabinet in the palace. On the wall opposite the
door is a small brass nailhead. Press it and a
little door will open, leading to my secret jew-
elry closet. Inside you will find the Seal."

Everyone was amazed at how the boy had
picked out Lord St. John. That lord, about to

"I Have the Perfect Test."

move, paused and looked at Tom, as if for permission.

"Why do you hesitate, St. John?" said Tom. "That was a command from the king."

Still unsure, St. John directed his bow to the space between the "two kings," then was gone. One by one, the nobles moved away from Tom and drifted over to the ragged boy's side.

Sir John returned and, with a deep bow to Tom, said, "Sire, the Seal is not there!"

The courtiers immediately hurried away from Edward as if he had the plague. Now he was the one left standing deserted.

"Throw the beggar into the street and whip him through the town!" called Lord Hertford.

But as the guards sprang to obey, Tom waved them away. "Back!" he cried. "Anyone who touches him risks his life!"

Again Hertford stood confused. He turned to St. John, saying, "How strange that something so big and bulky as that heavy gold disc should just disappear without. . . ."

"Anyone Who Touches Him Risks His Life!"

"Wait a minute!" Tom shouted. "Did you say a big and bulky round gold disc? Does it have letters and designs on it? Is *that* the Great Seal?"

"Yes, yes, My Lord," said Hertford. "Do you know where it is?"

"I do. But the true king shall tell you." He turned to Edward. "Think now. The last thing you did that day after we changed clothes was put it in a certain place."

Poor Edward shook his head. With his future at stake, he could not remember that one, single incident.

"Let me help you recall it as it happened," said Tom. "We were talking of my family in Offal Court. You gave me food and drink. Then we changed clothes. When we looked in the mirror and saw our resemblance to each other, you noticed that my hand had been hurt by your soldier, and you ran out to scold him. Remember? But just before you reached the door, you passed a table with this Seal on it.

"You Passed a Table with This Seal on It."

You picked it up and looked for a place to hide it —"

"Yes, yes, I recall!" cried Edward. "Now run, St. John, to the suit of Milanese armor on the wall. The Seal is in the armpiece!"

"Right, right, My King!" cried Tom. "Now the English throne is yours."

Frantic conversation burst forth as St. John left once again, but a sudden hush followed his return. He held up the Great Seal, and a mighty shout went up. "Long live the true king!"

Hertford eyed Tom angrily. "Let that young villain be stripped of his royal clothes and thrown into the Tower in rags!" he ordered.

But Edward cried out, "No! If not for him I would not have my crown again. And you, my good uncle, who schemed to get your new title, are no longer a duke. You are to remain an earl." Then turning to Tom, the king asked, "How was it you could remember where I hid the Great Seal and I could not?"

"Long Live the True King!"

"Because, Your Majesty, I used it on several occasions."

"You used it, yet you could not tell me where it was?"

"I didn't know *what* it was they were looking for. Nobody described it to me when they were looking for it."

"Then how did you use it?"

Tom blushed and was silent.

"Speak up, good Tom. Do not be afraid. Just how did you use the Great Seal of England?"

Tom stammered and, in confusion, finally got it out. "I-I used it to crack nuts."

The rush of laughter that followed nearly swept Tom off his feet. But his answer left no doubt in anyone's mind that Tom Canty was not the King of England.

Then the royal robes were removed from Tom's shoulders and placed around Edward's, covering his rags completely. The crowning ceremony went on as booming cannons thundered the news to all of London!

"I-I Used It To Crack Nuts."

The Whipping Boy Recognizes Miles.

CHAPTER 15

The Reunion

Meanwhile, Miles Hendon made his way out of the London Bridge mob, only to find that pickpockets had taken his last coin. He wandered through London, searching in vain for his poor, mad friend until, exhausted, he fell asleep in a doorway.

He awoke the next morning, famished, and decided to try to borrow some money from his late father's friend at court.

At eleven o'clock, he arrived at the palace gates, where he was spotted by the king's whipping boy, who recognized him immediately from a description the king had given him. "This tired soldier with the fancy, worn-out clothes is the very wanderer the king has been anxiously searching for," he thought. "I must speak to him."

But before the boy could say anything, Miles asked, "Since you have come from the palace, perhaps you know Sir Humphrey Marlowe?"

The boy stared and nodded. That was his own dead father.

"Please tell him that Miles Hendon, the son of his friend Sir Richard, wishes to see him."

"Wait right here, sir," said the boy, pointing to a bench.

Hardly was the boy out of sight when some guards seized Miles and charged him with prowling outside the palace grounds. "Disarm him and search him!" ordered an officer.

His men obeyed, but all they found was a bit of folded paper in his pocket. Miles smiled, remembering the day that his ragged little friend had scribbled the note in three languages

Guards Disarm and Search Miles.

at Hendon Hall. But his smile froze on hearing the guard read the English part.

"Another claimant to the throne!" shouted the officer. "Hold him while I take this note to the king!"

"Now I'll hang for sure!" thought Hendon. "And then what will happen to my poor boy?"

The officer came flying back and ordered Miles freed. He returned his sword and bowed respectfully, saying, "Please follow me, sir."

"If I were not so close to death and worried about sinning, Miles thought, "I'd strike him for mocking me with false politeness."

After a long walk through a great hall and up a broad staircase, they reached a huge room. The officer cleared a path through the masses of nobles, then left Miles standing, bewildered, in the middle of the floor.

The young king sat five steps away under a canopy, with his head turned aside, as he spoke with a nobleman. Miles wished the king would hurry and get the sentencing over with.

Standing Bewildered Before the King

THE PRINCE AND THE PAUPER

Just then, Edward raised his head and Miles got a good look at his face. The sight nearly took his breath away—for there, on a throne, was the Lord of the Kingdom of Dreams and Shadows! But all these elegant people here seemed real. "Is this a dream?" Miles asked himself, "or is he truly the King of England and not my poor, friendless lad?"

Suddenly, Miles came up with a way to answer the riddle. He walked over to a chair, picked it up, and plunked it down in front of the king. Then he sat in it!

A buzz of anger broke out in the room, and a rough hand shook his shoulder. "Get up, you clown!" said a firm voice. "No one is permitted to sit in the king's presence!"

"Let him alone!" ordered the king. "It is his right!"

The crowd fell back in amazement, as the king continued. "Lords and ladies all, I want you to know that this is my trusted and beloved servant, Miles Hendon. For using his

"Get Up, You Clown!"

sword to save his prince from bodily harm and possible death, he was made a knight. For saving his king from shame and a whipping, taking both upon himself, he was made an earl, the Earl of Kent. He shall now have the gold and lands that befit his title. And the right he just used is his by royal grant—the men of the Hendon line may sit in the presence of England's kings as long as there is a crown."

Two latecomers to the room stood listening and staring. They were Sir Hugh and Lady Edith. They were not noticed by the new Earl of Kent, who stood muttering, "And *this* is the poor, ragged boy I was going to impress with my seventy-room house! *This* is the mad boy I was going to cure and make respectable! Oh, how I wish I had a bag to hide my head in!" Then his manners came back, and he knelt and swore loyalty to the king.

As Miles rose and moved back toward the envious crowd, Edward's eyes caught sight of the pair from Hendon Hall. In an angry voice,

"He May Sit in the Presence of the King."

he ordered, "Take the stolen title and lands from this robber and lock him up."

As Hugh Hendon was led away, all eyes turned toward a boy who was being ushered in. It was Tom Canty, in a magnificent royal suit. The boy knelt before his king, who smiled as he spoke.

"I have heard all about how well you ruled these past few weeks, with gentleness and mercy . . . and how you have found your mother and sisters again. They will be cared for and, if you wish, your father will hang. I hereby order that from now on, the boys at Christ's Hospital be given an education along with their other needs. Tom Canty shall live there and be its board chief all his life.

"Also," continued Edward, "because he has been a king, he alone is to wear this special royal clothing. He is always to be treated with respect and be called by the honorable title of King's Ward, to show that he has the king's protection and support all his life."

Giving Tom the Title of King's Ward

Miles and Lady Edith Are Married.

CHAPTER 16

To a Better Life

The mysteries were all cleared up when Hugh Hendon admitted he had forced Lady Edith to pretend not to know Miles. He had threatened to have Miles killed unless she lied, and she had agreed, to save the man she loved.

Neither Lady Edith nor Miles would testify against Hugh, who left for France. He died there soon after. Miles, now the Earl of Kent, married Lady Edith, and the town rejoiced when the happy pair entered Hendon Hall.

John Canty was never heard from again.

Tom lived to be a wise old man, handsome and white-haired. Wherever he went, he was known by his special royal clothing. Crowds would make way, whispering, "Hats off! It's the King's Ward!" Tom would smile kindly in return, and the smile would mean something, coming from a man with an honorable history.

As for Edward VI, he lived only a few years, but he lived them well. He remembered and saved many of the victims he had met: the farmer who had been sold as a slave, the old imprisoned lawyer, the woman who had stolen some cloth, and the daughters of the two women he had seen burned at the stake. He also praised publicly the judge who had pitied him when he was accused of stealing a pig.

A few times, when some wealthy courtier complained that his laws were too easy, the young king would turn his kindly eyes on him and say, "What do you know of suffering and oppression? I and my people know, but not you!"

"I and My People Know of Suffering!"